BURYING GHOSTS

Publisher: *Mmap*
Mwanaka Media and Publishing Pvt Ltd
24 Svosve Road, Zengeza 1
Chitungwiza Zimbabwe
mwanaka@yahoo.com
mwanaka13@gmail.com
www.africanbookscollective.com/publishers/mwanaka-media-and-publishing
https://facebook.com/MwanakaMediaAndPublishing/

Distributed in and outside N. America by African Books
Collective
orders@africanbookscollective.com
www.africanbookscollective.com

ISBN: 978-1-77928-441-9
EAN: 9781779284419

DISCLAIMER
All views expressed in this publication are those of the author
and do not necessarily reflect the views of *Mmap*.

BURYING GHOSTS

Poetic Novel

Samuel Chuma

Mwanaka Media and Publishing Pvt Ltd,
Chitungwiza Zimbabwe
*
Creativity, Wisdom and Beauty

DEDICATION

This book is dedicated to my wife, Semina Hamandishe for love dedication and support during weather foul and fair.

Chapter 1: Father's House

The sun filtered softly through the Msasa trees that lined the edges of the homestead, casting mysterious patterns on the cracked red earth. These shapes always intrigued Ruramai. In quiet moments, she would speak with them. She called them her shadow friends, and in her young, uncluttered mind, she gave them pride of place.

These shadow beings were mostly friendly and unassuming, especially during the day when gently drawn by the sun's finger onto the canvas of her world. The sun, she thought, was a great democrat and leveler—it made no distinctions in its choice of canvas. It drew on walls, on the ground, rooftops, water. Even on fire.

Ruramai sometimes wished she were a shadow drawn by the sun. Then she wouldn't burn in fire, drown in water, or get swept away by the wind. What she envied most about the shadow people was their silence. They moved without noise, without screams, without blaring music—just one long peaceful quiet. Even the shadows in church, she noted, prayed silently. Unlike the congregation, who shouted as though God were deaf.

On this day, she ran barefoot across the yard, chasing her younger sister, Tari.

Tari was only six, smaller and more expressive, a flame that danced where Ruramai smoldered. She was fearless in ways that left adults anxious—she spoke boldly to strangers, questioned adults, and once attempted to ride a goat. She was utterly tactless with a motor-mouth and no social skills. Her laughter was uninhibited, echoing even when the day seemed heavy. She was the sort of child who believed her imagination could change reality—and hence occupied two worlds simultaneously; this one she shared with humanity, and the other one solely in her head. In that world she was both king and queen, slave and master and priest and fiend.

3

Ruramai giggled in pursuit, waving a rubber snake to scare her sibling. It was a strange item in their village—a toy so foreign it felt as out of place as a wedding ring on a thumb. But like everything else, it had its history.

Just as this land—her home, her country—boasted a history of its own. They said the story of the land was written in blood caked dusty idioms, with rifle bayonets and spears for pens, and writhing human bodies as the inkpot. Ruramai sometimes wondered if such a history could induce joy and laughter. But she quickly dismissed the thought. Those were adult matters, and her young mind had no business to linger there.

Her rubber snake, too, had its story.

A foreign donor organisation had gifted her school with prizes for outstanding students. Ruramai had been among the recipients.

She had walked proudly to the podium, her head held high, to the cheers of relatives and the envious glances of classmates. She curtsied, received her gift-wrapped box, opened it—and screamed. Then fainted.

Pandemonium broke out.

Her father reached her first, pushing others aside with a strength that was almost brutal. In the box, a life-like rubber green mamba stared back with such fierce indifference that even he recoiled. She was taken home on a rickety scotch cart with deflated wheels, dragged along the dusty path by an ageing ox too tired for urgency. It was the bumpy ride along the way that finally roused her to a confused wakefulness and by the time she got home, she was fully alert.

Hours later, she realized that someone had placed the box neatly by her school things. Her father explained gently that it was just rubber—nothing to fear.

But Ruramai had learned her lesson. In life, there were counterfeit things that felt real and caused real reactions. But they were fake all the same. Illusions. She would, from now on, learn to question before reacting. And if she reacted, she would not use that reaction as proof of a thing's truth. She would demand further validation. Always.

She often looked at the box and wondered—who thought such a gift would bring joy to a black African schoolgirl?

Still, she grew used to it. Grew attached to it. It became her constant companion. Just like the shadows: quiet, peaceful—unless misunderstood. Then, they became frightening and horrific.

She thought of her father.

Each morning, he sat on the veranda to greet the sun. He always rose before it. No matter the season, the sun never beat him. She once asked how he managed this.

"The sun is predictable," he said with a chuckle. "And unchangeable." Then he looked at her, eyes soft with parental love. "In life, never be predictable. Be a mystery. Don't be an open book."

He never raised his voice. Yet when he spoke, even the wind paused to listen. Ruramai adored him. Not only for his wisdom, but for his quiet strength and constant support.

He wasn't popular in the usual sense, but he was respected—deeply. Perhaps the community, unable to understand him, chose to err on the side of reverence. Not that he didn't deserve it. If ever a man did, it was him.

He was no one's friend, but also no one's enemy. Not unfriendly— just a contented introvert. He attended every funeral, every wedding, and every gathering where empathy or presence was expected.

He was not a snob.

"Do not fear the world," he once told her, cupping her small hand in his calloused palm. "But walk in it with your head up. No matter how loud it gets."

Those hands—rough and strong—were testaments to diligence. He did jobs others shunned: digging wells, clearing rubble, artisanal mining. Through sweat and toil, he secured a decent living for the family. They weren't rich, but they never lacked. Some even considered them comfortable.

There was always food on the table—natural, sumptuous meals. Because Father was a farmer.

After greeting the sun, he would take his hoe and head for the fields. His gait, like his nature, was deliberate. Never hurried, never frenzied—yet he covered ground faster than most. He was tall, muscular, his stride long and steady. Those legs made him a surprisingly fast walker.

Ruramai remembered being seven, crying and stumbling after him as he left home. He never looked back, never slowed. She hated him then—for not caring, for letting her suffer.

But her hate turned to determination. She pumped her aching legs faster, like miniature pistons, racing to catch him. And when she finally did, tugging at his trousers, he stopped.

He knelt, embraced her, kissed her forehead—and from some hidden pocket, pulled out her favourite lollipop. Then he hoisted her onto his shoulders.

In that moment, all anger melted. Only love remained. A deep indescribable and calming kind of affection.

Until the day Baba didn't return from the fields.

It had rained the night before. The grass was thick, the air damp. He left as usual—hoe in hand, stride purposeful. Hours later, a neighbor came running.

"He's been bitten," he cried.

They found him near the maize field, collapsed beside his hoe. One leg was swollen and darkened—a snake bite. A puff adder, they said.

There was no ambulance. No car. Only the rickety scotchcart, wheels long broken, dragged by the same tired ox. They placed him gently on it and pulled him home. He was still breathing then.

Mama screamed for help. For the healer. For anything. For the past.

But the past was gone.

Her grandfather, once a renowned healer of snake bites, had died years before. He had treated dozens, maybe hundreds, with roots, invocations, charms. But he had taken his knowledge with him. No notebook. No apprentice. No one left to remember.

Ruramai heard whispers in the dark: "If only Sekuru had taught someone..."

That was the danger of oral wisdom. When the tongue stills, knowledge dies. Traditions crumble. Secrets vanish. What had saved many in one generation left the next unarmed.

They tried everything. But his body shivered. Then stilled.

In the days that came, opinions split the village.

"Snakes are sacred," said a retired teacher from town. "They must be protected. They're shy, not aggressive. Puff adders are beautiful."

"Beautiful?" spat Aunt Rejoice. "Easy to say when your house is near a clinic."

"You want us to respect what kills us?" someone added. "Here, a bite is a death sentence."

Some nodded. Some did not.

To some, snakes were divine. Symbols of the ancestors. Part of the ecosystem.

To others, they were death with scales.

Ruramai listened. And remembered.

The dusty path where they carried his body. The stool by the door that remained empty. Tari, silent now, no longer chasing goats. Home, once filled with the smell of firewood and damp soil, now smelt of absence.

Chapter 2: The Stranger in Our Home

The rains came late that year, and the cracked earth seemed to cry for relief. In the same way, their household had grown brittle—held together by fragments of memory and quiet despair. Without Baba, everything felt temporary. Even time seemed unsure of itself.

The village of Gumbo, nestled between dry hills and dust-swept paths, seemed unchanged. But for Ruramai, the world had tilted. Since Baba's death, she had learned how long nights could be, how loud silence could roar. And how, even in a crowded room, grief could isolate you like a walled-off room.

Mama began to spend longer hours at the market, selling tomatoes, dried vegetables, and secondhand clothes. She returned late, her feet blistered, her eyes sunken, her laughter gone. Ruramai noticed the change—the way Mama began to talk less and sigh more. Her mother, once a quiet but steady flame, had dimmed to a flicker.

Tari, on the other hand, seemed untouched by the gravity of their loss. At six, she was joy in motion—loud, inquisitive, and stubborn. She still chased chickens, still tried to braid Ruramai's hair with clumsy fingers, still clapped her hands to the rhythm of her own singing. But even her brightness had begun to dim in recent weeks.

Then, one evening, Mama came home with a man.

His name was Gideon.

He was tall and broad, his voice booming like distant thunder, and his handshake deliberately firm. His skin was smooth, his scent sharp— a mix of musk and unfamiliar cologne. He wore pointed leather shoes that looked too expensive for the dust-covered village paths, and his laughter always arrived before he did.

"This is Uncle Gid," Mama said, trying to sound casual. "He helps me transport goods from town. He's just passing by."

But Uncle Gidzadidn't just pass by. He returned the next day. And the day after that. Then his toothbrush appeared by the sink. His boots by the door. His cup among the enamel ones. His laughter began to punctuate the evenings, mingling with the aroma of Mama's cooking. He was not a visitor. He was staking ground.

Gideon said he had worked in the city. He told stories of fast cars, noisy clubs, clever deals. He said he had grown tired of the city's lies and returned to the rural life to find peace. But everything about him—his manner, his tone, the way he watched things—seemed too polished, too rehearsed. He was from elsewhere, and the village was merely a pause, not a home.

To the community, he seemed like a godsend. A man had returned to restore what had been broken. Few questioned. Fewer cared. In places like Gumbo, a woman without a husband was considered incomplete. A family without a man was unfinished.

Mama, who had stopped singing, now hummed while she cooked. She laughed at Gideon's jokes, smiled as she served him sadza, and slowly began to speak more softly to her daughters. The house grew warmer—on the surface.

But Ruramai watched.

She saw how his eyes lingered on her a little too long. How his laughter paused when he looked at her. How his shadow sometimes passed too close to her bedroom door late at night. Her instincts, once quiet, now screamed.

Tari was too young to notice. She adored his stories about Harare's busy streets, the sweets he brought from town, and the way he called her "Little Boss." She followed him around the yard, giggling at his playful antics.

One night, Ruramai awoke to the curtain in her room shifting gently. She was sure she had closed it. She lay still, breath shallow, heart pounding. And then she saw the shadow retreat.

She didn't tell Mama.

Another time, while bathing behind the hut, she felt the prickle of a gaze. She turned. He stood at a distance, pretending to check the tether on a goat. He didn't speak. He only smiled.

Still, she said nothing.

Mama began referring to him as Baba Gid. The name took root quickly. Tari said it easily. Mama said it softly. And the village accepted it without question. What was once unspoken became settled fact.

Then one Sunday afternoon, Mama called her into the kitchen.

"Rura," she said while stirring a pot slowly, "Gidza wants to help with your school fees. Isn't that a blessing?"

Ruramai nodded, a motion that cost her more than words.

"Life is not easy without a man," Mama continued. "Sometimes we must accept help when it comes. Even if it doesn't come in the way we expected."

Her words carried weight. Not a lesson. A warning. A plea.

That night, Ruramai lay under her blanket, unable to sleep. Tears traced silent paths down her cheeks. She clutched the memory of her father tightly—his voice, his scent, the calm in his footsteps. She dreamt of him that night. In the dream, he sat beneath the Msasa tree, beckoning her with a smile. But when she ran to him, the ground cracked open, and he disappeared into shadow.

She began withdrawing into herself.

Her words became few. Her laughter, rare. At school, she threw herself into her studies, determined to carry on what Baba had begun. She remembered how he always said education was the only inheritance that couldn't be stolen.

At night, while Mama and Gideon slept inside, she sat outside under the stars, revising her textbooks by the flicker of a paraffin lamp. She stopped playing with Tari. She stopped asking questions. She began stepping into the shoes Baba had left behind—comforting Tari, collecting firewood, budgeting the few coins Mama left behind. She wasn't the child anymore.

10

She had become something else. A custodian. A protector. A child heading a household.

Her body, too, was changing. One afternoon at school, she felt a dull ache in her belly and a slow wetness that made her panic. In the pit latrine, she found the blood. Her first period. Her initiation into womanhood came with neither celebration nor guidance. Just confusion, shame, and a makeshift pad fashioned from toilet paper and newspaper.

That evening, she didn't tell anyone. But she walked a little differently. Sat a little straighter. Something had shifted. Her childhood was gone.

With the physical change came emotional heat—a newfound awareness of her body, of glances, of her own presence in space. She found herself observing older girls, noticing their curves, their laughs, the way they swung their hips with quiet pride. She studied them silently, wondering if she would ever feel that confident.

One boy at school, Tapiwa, caught her attention. He was soft-spoken and always seemed to stand up when others mocked the weak. He once lent her a pencil without asking for it back. She began to notice the way his hand gripped the pen, how his eyes narrowed in concentration.

She didn't talk to him. But in her dreams, he held her hand. In her notebook margins, she scribbled his name next to hearts.

It was innocent, her first crush. A whisper of what love might one day feel like. It gave her something private, something soft to hold on to. Her fantasy was not of kisses or embraces, but of being understood, of someone listening and saying, "I see you."

In Gumbo, that wasn't rare. There were others like her—children who bore adult burdens, who cooked and cleaned and hid tears from younger siblings. They were not pitied. They were the norm.

And so, while the village celebrated Mama's new man, Ruramai wore her grief like an invisible shawl. Heavy. Warming nothing.

And the stranger in their home, who now slept in her father's place, was no longer a guest.

He was family.

Chapter 3: The Quiet Rebellion

The sun had not yet risen, but the sky glowed faintly, like a secret being whispered to the morning. Ruramai stood outside with a bundle of firewood on her head and a sour taste in her mouth that had nothing to do with hunger. The earth beneath her was damp with dew. The birds were still deciding whether or not to sing.

She had not slept well.

It was becoming routine now—these restless nights, filled with the murmur of wind and the creak of the old wooden door. Her body had adjusted to waking before everyone else, to boiling water in silence, to hearing her mother's muffled laughter from behind the curtain that separated their room from Gideon's. Each sound had become a sentence in a book she no longer wanted to read.

Mama was changing. Where there had once been a sharpness in her eye and a quiet resistance in her walk, there was now something soft and contented, like a warm towel. Her voice rose in a new octave when she spoke to Gideon. She seemed to lean toward him even when standing. It pained Ruramai to see the transformation—not because her mother did not deserve to smile, but because the smile had been bought too cheaply.

Gideon had begun to give orders. First small ones: "Tari, fetch my shoes." "Rura, clean this cup." But gradually, the tone shifted. There was something proprietary in the way he moved, like the house and all in it belonged to him. And perhaps, in Mama's eyes, it did.

Ruramai complied, but quietly. She had learned the art of invisibility—to float through the day like a feather, light, silent, and careful not to catch the wind. But inside her, something was hardening. It wasn't anger. Not yet. It was understanding.

She was becoming a woman.

Her breasts were budding beneath her blouses, and boys at school had started to look at her differently. Their teasing carried a new tone, laced with curiosity. Some days it made her smile in secret. Other days it made her fold into herself like a seed seeking safety.

Tapiwa, her soft-spoken classmate, remained kind. They had exchanged more words now, cautious and measured, like stepping stones across a fast river. He had once offered to carry her books, and she had let him. Their fingers brushed. Neither spoke of it, but they both remembered.

They began to walk part of the way home together, feet kicking loose gravel, talking about things that didn't seem to matter until they did—weather, teachers, who had cheated on the math test. Once, he told her he thought she'd make a good lawyer. It made her heart beat strangely, proudly.

One day, after school, he gave her a page torn from his own notebook. On it, he had written a short poem. About a girl with sharp eyes and silent strength. He didn't name her, but she knew. She tucked the page into her uniform blouse and didn't tell anyone.

She began to dream of other places. Not just escape, but becoming—a woman with purpose. A teacher. A writer. Someone whose voice mattered. She wrote in secret. Her father's old exercise books, their pages yellowed and curled at the edges, became her diary. There, she wrote poems. Thoughts. Prayers. She addressed them all to Baba.

"Baba, today I helped Tari with her sums. She is clever. I think she gets that from you."

"Baba, Mama laughed today. I wanted to be happy for her. I tried."

"Baba, I think I am disappearing. Sometimes I feel like a chair. Everyone sits on me, and when they get up, I stay there. Silent. Waiting."

Her words became her rebellion. Her quiet rebellion.

At school, she studied harder than ever. She ranked top of her class in English and History. Her teacher, Mrs. Mandaza, called her "a sponge with a soul." She began staying behind after school to help clean the classroom, not because she had to, but because the silence there was different—not heavy like home, but open, waiting to be filled with possibility.

One Friday afternoon, after most of the class had gone, Mrs. Mandaza approached her.

"Ruramai, what do you want to be?"

She hesitated.

"I don't know yet, but I want to speak. To say things that matter."

The teacher nodded, eyes kind. "Then keep writing. Keep reading. One day, someone will listen."

That night, Ruramai stayed up longer than usual, scribbling by candlelight. Her fingers cramped, but her soul stretched. In her notebook, she wrote:

"I am the daughter of a quiet man. I will not shout. But I will speak."

Saturdays were long and filled with chores. She fetched water in heavy buckets, her spine aching but her mind humming with thoughts. As she swept the yard, she narrated stories to herself in whispers. A girl who outwitted monsters. A girl who planted truth where lies had once grown. These were stories she never wrote down, but they were her fuel.

At the grinding mill, where women gossiped and men smoked in shadows, she often heard whispers about her mother. "She has found a man." "She is lucky." "The girl needs to be tamed before she embarrasses her mother."

She heard it all.

And she smiled.

Because if they feared her quietness, they hadn't seen her strength.

Back home, Gideon had begun to drink more. Not every day. But when he did, the house changed shape. The air grew tense, like it was holding its breath. Mama laughed less. Tari clung to Ruramai more often. And Ruramai's instincts sharpened like a blade.

One evening, he stumbled home with a sour scent and red eyes.

15

"Rura, where is my plate?"

She brought it without a word. He ate noisily, bones cracking, lips smacking.

When she turned to go, he grabbed her wrist. Too tight.

"You think you're better than us, neh? With your books and your English?"

She met his gaze. Calm. Cold. Silent.

He let her go, scowling.

Later that night, she packed her exercise books into a cloth bag and hid them under her bed.

She was not going to be broken.

She was not going to be silenced.

She would endure. But she would also prepare.

Because rebellion was not always fire and shouts. Sometimes, it was a girl with a dream, a notebook, and a quiet, burning will.

Chapter 4: The Things We Carry

Grief doesn't leave. It settles. It shifts shape, puts on new clothes, changes its scent—but it never really leaves. Ruramai learned this the way one learns drought—not from a single dry day, but from the slow yellowing of leaves, the hardening of the ground beneath bare feet.

And the flight of life.

By the time the August winds arrived, whistling through the Mopani trees and lifting skirts and raising dust and tempers alike, life in the household had congealed into something unspoken. Something dark black. It wasn't harmony. But it was balance—of the uneasy, fragile sort.

Tari had stopped asking questions about Baba. She now called Gideon "Baba Gid" without hesitation. She had grown used to the presence, the voice, the gruff commands.

Ruramai hadn't.

But she had learned to nod without listening, to obey without agreement.

To move through the house like smoke.

Unseen, unrestricted.

School was her sanctuary. It remained the only space where she felt herself expand, not shrink. The classroom smelled of chalk and hope, the rows of desks etched with the history of children who had come before her—

Some dreamers.

Some rebels.

Some simply trying to survive.

Ruramai sat near the window, where light touched her notes and birds reminded her that not everything was trapped.

Her teacher, Mrs. Mandaza, took a keen interest in her. After school, they spoke more often—about books, yes, but also about the world

17

beyond the village. About Harare. Universities. Scholarships. Mrs. Mandaza had been educated abroad. She once brought in a novel and placed it gently in Ruramai's hands.

"You must learn to imagine more than survival," she said. "The world is wide, *asikana*. Let it stretch you."

At home, that stretch became resistance.

She began writing more fervently—tucking poems beneath her mattress, scribbling thoughts on the back of old receipts. Her diary had grown fat with feeling.

Each entry a balm.

Each page a small rebellion.

Gideon, meanwhile, grew meaner in silence. He no longer pretended. He drank more openly. He sulked when spoken to, barked when not. His moods were like storms—unpredictable, destructive, and, worst of all, expected.

One Sunday, after church, they returned home to find him sprawled on the veranda. The smell preceded him. He sat with legs wide, a bottle resting against his thigh, his eyes bloodshot and unfocused.

"Late, as usual," he slurred, not looking at them.

Mama clutched Tari's hand and walked past him without a word. Ruramai followed, carrying the Bible and the leftover rice in a tied plastic bag.

But he followed. Stumbling. Insistent.

"Woman, I'm hungry!" he shouted. "What kind of wife doesn't prepare her man's food?"

He kicked a stool. It splintered.

Tari whimpered.

Mama moved to shield her, but he was faster. He grabbed the edge of the cooking pot and flung it across the yard. Its contents scattered like accusations.

Then he raised his hand.

It didn't land.

Ruramai stood in the way.

She didn't speak. She just stared.

The moment hung. Even the wind paused. It was as though the house, the trees, and the world held its breath.

He faltered. Then cursed. Then left.

That night, he didn't sleep in the house. They heard him pacing outside, muttering, and drinking.

That was the night something shifted in Mama too.

The next morning, she rose early. She boiled water, cleaned the yard, made porridge. But her eyes were elsewhere. Focused. Alert.

She began saving scraps. Dried meat wrapped in cloth. Coins folded into the hems of her skirt. She whispered more with Aunt Fadzi on the phone. And once, Ruramai saw her carefully folding a paper with numbers on it. A bus timetable. From Zaka to Harare.

She didn't explain. But she didn't need to.

Ruramai understood. They were no longer just tolerating.

They were preparing.

At night, Ruramai began to draw a map in her mind. A map of what-ifs and maybes. She envisioned a future where she studied law. Where she walked confidently through a city street. Where she wrote stories that mattered.

In one of her poems, she wrote:

"We carry many things—
Bread asleep in baskets.
Secrets growling in stomachs.
And sometimes,
A whole revolution
Crouched beneath the tongue."

Tari had become quieter too. She clung to Ruramai more, asked to sleep in her bed more often. One night, when thunder rolled in the distance, she whispered, "Do you think Baba Gidza loves us?"

Ruramai didn't answer.

But she held her tight.

Weeks passed. The wind howled louder. The days grew hotter. There were fewer smiles in the house.

Then, one Friday morning, Gideon announced he was leaving for a few days.

"Going to see a cousin in Bikita," he said, eyes scanning Mama.

No one responded.

He left with a bag and two empty bottles in his hand.

As soon as his figure disappeared into the bush, Mama locked the door.

She turned to Ruramai.

"Pack only what matters."

That night, they didn't sleep. They whispered. They wrapped clothes in grain bags. They boiled eggs and folded paper money into soap bars. They prepared.

In the early morning, just as the rooster crowed, they left.

Past the graveyard. Where father lay. He didn't wave goodbye.

But he didn't stop them either.

Past the school. Down the path that curved like memory itself.

They carried only what they needed.

And what they couldn't carry, they left buried—in earth, in silence, in verse.

And in an unkempt of the mind's cemetery.

Ruramai looked back only once.

The house stood still. Silent. Emptied of everything except for ghosts.

But in her chest, something beat loudly. Not fear.

Something wilder.

Freedom.

They walked toward the bus stop, three women—one grown, one growing, one girl.

Carrying pain.

Carrying hope.

Carrying each other.

Sometimes, it was the way she held her head at assembly. The way she refused to cry. The way she looked beyond the hut and the hills and saw, not escape, but something she could build with her own hands.

Ruramai's rebellion had no name yet. But it had roots. And a heart that beat.

And like any seed buried deep in the dark, it was already reaching for the light.

Chapter 5: Cities Don't Save You

The bus wheezed. Coughed. Groaned like an old man trying to stand. It carried them forward. Away.

Ruramai watched the land flatten into tremulous heat. The sky sagged. Mopani trees thinned out. The air changed its accent. It lost its stammer like Moses before Pharaoh.

Behind them—earth, grief, a broken stool.

Where aborted dreams fought for a seat.

And forgot to wave goodbye.

Ahead—noise.

The journey wasn't quiet. Babies cried. Women shouted prices for boiled eggs and boiled nuts imprisoned in plastic. A man preached with wild eyes, thumping a worn Bible as if berating it for some evil deed done in secret that only he knew.

Mama said nothing. Her jaw was set. Eyes hard. Like she had swallowed her own voice.

Tari slept. One hand on Ruramai's thigh. The other curled near her mouth, fingers twitching in a dream. With a smile on her face.

Not peaceful.

But strange.

Ruramai wrote with her mind. Not on paper. The bus bumps wouldn't allow it.

You can leave a man.
But not his voice.
It follows.
Like a fart.
Like shame.

When they reached the city, it didn't rise like a promise. It sprawled. It snarled. Waved its tail. And barked.

It smelled of diesel and meat smoke and urine and something else—fleas, maybe.

Harare didn't welcome them.

It swallowed them.

At Mbare Musika, the crowd flowed like water. Fast. Relentless. Touts pulled bags and promises. Chickens flapped in crates. A man pissed against a wall while reading the newspaper. Nobody looked twice.

Mama held tight. "Keep moving."

They found Aunt Fadzi in a narrow corridor smelling of boiled cabbage and unwashed ambition. Her room was small. Cramped. But warm. Ruramai remembered her perfume—strawberries and danger.

That night they slept.

In a pile. Legs tangled. Hearts racing.

For the first time in years, there was no shouting. No thrown pots. No smell of beer soaking into floorboards. No dripping urine from the mattress.

Just an infant peace.

But peace too has its own violence.

It makes space for thoughts.

And thoughts can stab.

Fadzi worked nights. She wore short skirts and long eyelashes. She brought back chips, gossip, sometimes blood on her heels. But she never judged.

"Men are men," she said once. "And survival has no manners."

Ruramai didn't ask what she meant.

She understood anyway.

Mama tried to be invisible. She woke early. Scrubbed the stairwell. Sold boiled peanuts in a frayed reed basket. Her eyes stopped blinking when spoken to. They just stared. Measuring people. Closing her mind's curtains. Deciding who to trust.

Tari missed school. She played with bottle caps. She drew stick people on the wall with charcoal. She called all dolls "Mama."

One afternoon, she looked up and asked, "Do all men shout?"

Ruramai didn't answer.

But later, she ripped a page from her diary and wrote:

If kindness is a coat,
Why do so many men dance naked?

School was no longer simple. The city school wanted documents. Letters. Fees. Faces that looked like they belonged.

They had none of those.

Ruramai sat on the landing most days, scribbling on brown paper bags. Writing helped. It made the world make sense. It turned fear into form.

One boy, nose crusted and eyes too old, pointed at her notebook. "You write poems?"

She nodded.

"Write about us," he said. "People like us disappear unless ink remembers."

That night she tried.

But the words wouldn't come.

Only silence.

And silence is hard to embrace.

Mama cut her hair.

Slowly. In the sink. With kitchen scissors.

Each strand dropped like a sentence being erased.

Tari watched, wide-eyed.

Ruramai stood in the doorway. She wanted to cry. But didn't.

Hair is history.

When it's gone, you feel colder.

Mama looked in the mirror and didn't smile. But she didn't flinch either.

"Gideon won't recognize me," she said.

It wasn't a question.

It was a declaration.

Fadzi warned them one night. A whisper, sharp as a blade.

"He's looking."

Mama froze. "You saw him?"

"No. But people talk. Men like him don't lose face quietly."

The next morning, they packed again.

Not to leave.

But to be ready.

Always ready.

Ruramai started walking differently. Quieter. Tighter. Like she might have to run again.

She began sleeping with a small knife under her pillow. The handle smooth. The metal cool against her skin.

She told no one.

But in her diary, she wrote:

Freedom is not the absence of fear.
It is walking anyway.
With your hands shaking.
With your eyes open.
With your past dragging behind you like a wounded dog.

Cities don't save you.

They give you corners to hide in. Skirts to hold. Smoke to blend into.

But not safety.

Not peace.

Just space.

Space to mutate. To become something else.

Even a cancerous tumor.

Or nothing at all.

Ruramai wasn't sure which she wanted.

But she kept writing.

Because stories are anchors.

Because paper listens better than people.

Because sometimes, a girl with ink-stained fingers is more dangerous than a man with a bottle.

Chapter 6: The Shape of Hunger

Harare spread beneath them like a wound that had learned how to walk. Tall buildings, potholed streets oozing sewage, tired houses and plastic cabins slunk into view. The city didn't rise—it crouched. Watching. Waiting. Licking its mouth.

The women moved through it like whispers. Three shadows. One hope.

They didn't speak of Gideon. Not aloud. But he was there. In the way Mama jumped at motorbike revs. In the way Ruramai stopped smiling when a man asked the time. In the way Tari clung tighter every time the door rattled.

Safety was a performance. They wore it like borrowed coats. Too big. Too itchy. Full of bedbugs.

In Aunt Fadzi's flat, time melted. The days bled into each other. There were no clocks, only the sound of children running down corridors, the groan of water pipes, and the scrape of spoons in empty pots.

Mama found work cleaning offices. Early mornings. Late nights. Her back bent further with every shift. Her silence thickened. She stopped humming. She stopped looking Ruramai in the eye.

Some nights, she came home with a bruised lip.

Sometimes a black eye.

Sometimes a limp.

Sometimes all three.

And said it was from a door. Nobody asked more.

Ruramai began walking. Not for errands. For understanding. She walked through Mbare, Highfields, Epworth, Kuwadzana. She watched women balancing buckets like crowns, men shouting at football matches watched on betting shops TVs, children dancing to music from cracked phones.

Everywhere was hunger.
Not just for food. For dignity. For kindness. For breath.
And sometimes for death.
At a street corner, she met a girl with cornrows and a laugh like gravel slithering in a metal gutter.
"You look like you read a lot," the girl said.
Ruramai shrugged.
"I'm Charity. You wanna see something real?"
She followed. Through alleys, into a room lit by candle ends and decorated with graffiti prayers. There, teenagers read poems aloud. Angry ones. Tender ones. Bleeding ones.
A boy named Tinaye read a piece that started:

My mother died with her dreams still folded in the wardrobe.
My father wore them to a brothel.

Ruramai didn't clap. She stared. And something inside her burst. Not broken. Just open.
When it was her turn, she read nothing. Just stood.
The others didn't push. They knew silence was a voice.
That night, she wrote a new poem. In ink. With purpose.

The city is a stomach.
It digests the brave.
Spits out bones.
But I am not bones.
I am fire chewing its way out.

Mama grew sharper. Her eyes darted more. She counted coins three times. She whispered to herself.

One morning, she forgot Tari at home. Just walked off. Ruramai found her on a park bench hours later, shoes off, face blank.

"I forgot I had children," Mama said.

They sat in silence. Leaves fell. The air smelt of smoke and roast maize.

Tari began wetting the bed. Every night.

Fadzi grew tense. She smoked more. Swore louder.

"This is no life," she snapped one night. "We survive and survive and for what? So the men who broke us can sleep soundly while we dream of knives?"

Ruramai started collecting voices. Recording the city in phrases and scents.

Sweat and polish.

Fried kapenta and boiled sorrow.

Laughter that peeps from behind teeth.

She stitched these into her notebook like spells.

Then came the news.

Gideon had been seen.

Not in Mbare. Not near them.

But too close.

Fadzi told them in a hush. Mama dropped a mug. It shattered. Became fragments.

Nobody moved to piece it together again. Same as broken dreams, And torn hymens.

That night, Ruramai stayed awake. Knife in hand. Pulse loud. She dreamt of fire. Smoke.

And a laughing Fire Department truck.

When morning came, she wrote:

We didn't escape.
We just changed cages;
No freedom even in perfumed jails

At the youth poetry meetings, she read for the first time. Her voice didn't tremble. Tinaye watched her like she was wind. Charity cheered too loud.

Afterward, he walked her home.

"You write like war," he said.

She smiled. Not because it was true.

But because someone had seen.

He kissed her. Light. Nervous.

She didn't flinch.

Later, alone, she wrote:

Even cracked soil grows things.

Mama lost her job.

Too many missed shifts. Too much silence.

She stayed in bed for three days. Fadzi yelled. Cried. Then gave up.

Ruramai took her poems to a community paper. Asked if they'd publish. The editor squinted.

"You're young. But fierce."

He gave her a column. Unpaid. But read.

Her words became ink.

Sometimes, survival is not noble.

It's just what you do because dying feels too quiet. And too boring.

People began to notice.

A teacher from a school in Glen View offered her a scholarship.
She started wearing shoes again.
Not because she needed to.
But because it felt like choosing.

Gideon did not come. Not as yet.
But they lived like he might.
Always half-packed. Always watching.
But now, they had something more than fear.
They had words.
And words, Ruramai learned, were not just stories.

They were teeth.
They were wings.
They were prisons.

Chapter 7: What We Call Ours

You can live somewhere for months.
Eat its bread.
Breathe its smoke.
Smell its shit.
Know the names of its stray dogs—
and still not belong.

Harare hadn't claimed them.
Not yet.
It watched them.
Tolerated them.
Like lions in zoos. Who have learnt how to unlock their cages?

But they were learning to move through its pulse.
To walk faster.
Talk less.
Watch more.

Mama sat by the window most days now.
Not watching anything in particular.
Just sitting.
One hand in her lap.
The other touching the soft part of her neck—where Gideon once left a bruise that lasted two weeks.

Ruramai noticed her fading.
The way some stars just go quiet.
Not explode.
Not cry.
Just—stop.

Tari hummed now.
Tuneless.
Endless.
Songs only she knew.
Sometimes she would draw circles.
On paper.
On walls.
In the air.

When asked what they were, she said, "Homes."

Ruramai wrote every night.

Sometimes by candlelight.
Sometimes by the glow of the city leaking through the curtain.
Always by memory.

Her column was catching fire.
Not fame.
Not fortune.
But murmurs.
People called her "the girl with the switchblade poems."
She didn't correct them.

She liked the danger in that.

One day, she came home to find a letter on the floor.

Opened.
Read.
Fingerprints in the fold.

It was from a publisher.
They wanted her words.
Wanted more.

Mama hadn't looked at it.
But Ruramai knew Fadzi had.

She confronted her.

"I just wanted to be sure it wasn't a trick," Fadzi said. "You can't trust men who want things."

Ruramai didn't shout.
She just walked to the sink.
Ran water over her hands.
Slow. Cold.

Then she said, "This is mine."

Tinaye kissed her behind the old bakery.
Her back against the red bricks.
His breath warm with fermented *maheu* and dreams.

She kissed him back.

Not because she needed to.

But because she wanted to feel something that didn't come with bruises.

Afterward, they lay on flour sacks.
And spoke of tomorrows.

He wanted to paint.
She wanted to write louder.

"Let's burn this whole city with our names," he whispered.

She smiled.
Not because it was true.
But because it could be.

Gideon returned in her dreams first.

Louder.
Angrier.
Sometimes gentler—
which scared her more.

Dreams are liars.

Mama's silence became thicker.
Like fog.
Like secrets under the tongue.

Ruramai asked her once,
"What do you want?"

Mama blinked.
Tari sneezed in the next room.
Fadzi coughed.

Then Mama said, "To be a woman again. Not a wound."

Tari was growing.
Not taller.
But inward.

She'd sit under the table and whisper to a stone she carried in her pocket.

"Baba Gidza won't find us," she'd say.

Ruramai didn't tell her that stones don't protect.

But she began writing poems for her.

Soft ones.
Bright ones.
On colored paper when she could find it.

She placed them under her pillow at night.

Tari called them "dream guards."

One afternoon, Ruramai walked past a burning pile of clothes.

Old uniforms.
School shoes.
A belt.
A girl stood nearby, hands folded.

"Starting over," she said.

Ruramai nodded.
Understood.

She went home and threw away all her old drafts.
The angry ones.
The ones soaked in Gideon's name.

Started new pages.
Clean.
Sharp.

Wrote:

Not all girls survive.
But the ones who do—
We tie nations
Around our waists
And dance the maddening dance

The landlord raised the rent.

Fadzi exploded.
A pan flew.
A word broke.
A door slammed.

They had a week to find somewhere new.

Nowhere safe.
Nowhere cheap.

So they moved into a building without windows.
Just holes.
Graffiti.
And a boy downstairs who played mbira for his dead brother.

The new place stank of decayed honour and impatient secrets.

They simply called it "The Place."

Because calling it "home" was too generous.

Ruramai stopped checking behind her.

Stopped flinching when footsteps echoed.

She still carried the knife.
But it wasn't for Gideon anymore.

It was for remembering who she had become.

Her poems changed.
Less pain.
More resistance.
More fire.

One night, she read in front of a full room.

Tinaye filmed it.

She said:

We are not your shadows.
We are storms that learned to walk
Without tiptoeing.

The crowd roared.

Mama was there.

In the back.
Arms folded.
Eyes glassy.

After the show, she hugged her.

Not hard.
Not long.

But real.

"I see you now," she whispered.

And that was the night Ruramai realized—

She wasn't running anymore.

She was rising.

Chapter 8: The Echo of Names

Gideon returned like a smell you thought you'd caged in perfume.
Like sweat soaked into wood.
Like semen stains on a mattress.

Not loud.
Not drunk.
Not wild.

He came back sober— which was worse.

The first whisper came from the woman who sold contraceptives and condoms on the corner. At the church gate.

"He was asking. Said he had business in the area."

Then a boy who cleaned car windows and stole from motorists said, "A man with a limp. He looked lost. But his eyes—his eyes were hunting."

Then silence.

The kind of silence that tightens a throat.
Wraps itself around a family.
And waits.
Mama dropped the tomatoes.

They rolled.
Bright.
Embarrassed.

She didn't pick them up.
Didn't blink.
Just stood there.

A woman tried to hand them back.
Mama walked away.

Later, Ruramai found her sitting on the floor.
Still wearing her shoes.
Hands shaking, but dry.

"I thought we were done with him," she whispered.

Ruramai knelt.
Tari watched from behind the curtain.

Nobody said anything else.

Fadzi was all rage.

"You should have killed him when you had the chance," she spat.

Ruramai didn't ask when that chance had been.
She just watched her aunt dig through drawers for a padlock, a screwdriver, a hammer.

Tari stopped humming for three days.

She drew a house with no doors.
No windows.
Just three hearts inside.

The city changed again.

The light felt different.
The air felt watched.

Ruramai began checking reflections.
Windows.
Spoons.
Shiny tiles.

Always expecting to see him there.
A shadow with her name tattooed on its tongue.

She tried writing.

Her pen stuttered.

Words fled the page like ants disturbed.

Tinaye noticed first.

"You're quieter," he said.
They were sitting on a bench.
Watching the traffic like it owed them something.

"I'm sharpening," she replied.

He didn't ask more.
He held her hand.

Gently.
Like she was made of stories.

The next time Gideon came, he didn't knock.

He stood by the gate.

Waited.

Watched.

Mama was cooking.

The smell of sadza and rape.

Fadzi saw him through the curtain.

"That bastard," she hissed.

She didn't go out.

She called Ruramai instead.

"What do we do?"

Ruramai didn't hesitate.

"We don't open."

That night, she wrote again.

Some men return as ghosts.

Some return as gods.
And some return as men who need to be reminded they are neither.

She folded the page.

Slid it into her shoe.

Then she lit a candle.

She told Tinaye,
"I'm speaking tomorrow."

He nodded.
Didn't ask what about.
He already knew.

The poetry venue was packed.

Girls with earrings like portals to the afterlife.
Boys with notebooks panting with rage.
Mothers who had stories but no tongues.

Ruramai stood behind the mic.

It smelled like metal and breath.

She didn't flinch.

She became the microphone.

"My name is not what he called me," she began.

"My name is what he stole."

"But still I remember. My name is Ruramai."

*"He said love.
But meant dominance."*

*"He said father.
But meant repression."*

The room held its breath.

"I refuse to carry his scars anymore."

Pause.

"Let him carry his own shame."

"I puke it back."
The crowd didn't cheer.

Not right away.

They just stood.

Hands to mouths.
Eyes wet.

Then someone clapped.

Then everyone did.

It wasn't applause.
It was thunder.

The next morning, the newspaper came.

Her poem in bold black.

"When Fathers Fail and Daughters Burn."

People stopped her in the street.

"You wrote this?"
"Is it true?"
"Are you safe?"

She nodded.

But didn't answer.

Gideon came one last time.

Tried to stand outside the gate again.

Fadzi walked out with a bucket.

Threw old mop water at his shoes.

"Next time," she said, "it won't be water."

He walked away.

Didn't come back.

But Ruramai knew—

It wasn't over.

Only paused.

That night, Mama spoke.

She came to Ruramai's bed.

Sat down.

Held her hand.

"I saw the paper," she said.

"I'm sorry I wasn't the mother I was supposed to be."

Ruramai didn't speak.

Mama continued.

"He killed more than your voice. He killed my courage too."

Silence.

Then:

"But you—
you brought it back."

In the other room, Tari whispered to her stone.

But now, her voice was louder.

"Baba Gidza is gone," she said.

The stone didn't reply.

It didn't need to.

Chapter 9: Blood Does Not Bend

He came in the morning.

Not with fists.

With flowers.

Bought from a street child, their petals tired, their stems thirsty.

He stood at the gate.
Again.
Again.
Again.

This time, Mama saw him first.

She didn't speak.

Just stared.

Then said, "Let him wait."

The flat went quiet.

Tari crawled under the table.

Fadzi poured tea, hands shaking just enough to spill.
Then said, "Coward's trying charm now."

Ruramai stood in the corner.

Listening to the silence between heartbeats.

Her hands were dry.
Her mouth bitter.

She walked out.

Not slow.
Not fast.
Just straight.

The sun blinked.
Birds held their notes.
The city leaned in.

He turned.

Her name spilled from him like wine.

"Ruramai."

She said nothing.

He tried again.
Voice soft.
False sugar.

"You look well."

She said nothing.

"You've grown into—"
"Stop."

He did.

The street held its breath.

"I'm sorry," he said.

She tilted her head.

"What are you sorry for?"
"For... for hurting you."
"Say it."
"I—"
"Say it."

His lips trembled.

"I raped you."

Someone down the street dropped a bucket.

Water splashed.

A baby wailed.

Still, Ruramai didn't blink.

She stepped forward.

And spoke.

"You took something that was not yours."

"You turned love into mucus."

"You turned a house into a mouth full of knives."

"You made my mother small."

"You made me silent."

"You made my sister draw houses with no doors."

"And now you want to return?"

He shook.
Whether from shame or wind—she couldn't tell.

"Please," he whispered.

"I just want a second chance."

"God forgives."

Ruramai stepped closer.

The flowers crumbled in his hand.

"I am not God," she said.

Then, softer.

"But I see him now."

Gideon looked up.

Eyes wet.

"You're not him either."

"You're just a man who was never taught how to bleed properly."

She turned.

Walked away.

Every step louder than his breathing.

Every heartbeat heavier than his apology.

Mama was at the window.

Fadzi held the door.

Tari peeked from the curtain.

And for the first time—

They all exhaled together.

That night, Mama spoke.

"I married him because I was tired of scraping for dignity."

"I stayed because I thought silence would save us."

"I was wrong."

Ruramai didn't comfort her.

She placed a cup of tea in her hand.

Sat beside her.

And let the quiet do its work.

Tinaye came later.

With oranges.

And music.

He held her like she was still whole.

"I heard," he said.

She nodded.

"I didn't kill him," she said.

Tinaye smiled.

"Good."

"You didn't need to."

The paper called again.

Asked if she wanted to write an essay.

"On fatherhood," they said.

She laughed.

Then wrote:

Blood does not bend.
It breaks.
It bruises.
It builds, sometimes, but only if you water it with truth.

55

Fadzi threw a party.

Small.

Loud.

Cheap wine and stolen music.

Women came.
Women who had scars and stories.

They danced.

Mama even smiled.

For the first time in years, she smiled without apology.

In the middle of the laughter, Ruramai stood.

Held a glass.

Tapped it.

The room stilled.

She said:

"To those who left."

"To those who stayed."

"To those who screamed."

"To those who whispered."

"To those who lived, even if they didn't want to."

"And to us."

The room raised their glasses.

"To us."

Later, Fadzi kissed her cheek.

"You didn't just survive, baby. You remade the whole script."

Ruramai leaned into the hug.

But her eyes were far away.

On the sky.
On the moon.
On the space between galaxies.

Where freedom sleeps. Snoring.

Chapter 10: The Things We Choose

The envelope came folded and white.
Thin paper. Thick consequence.

Ruramai didn't open it right away.

She stared at it.
Like it might explode.
Like it already had.

She held it in both hands.
As if her life needed cradling.

When she finally tore it open, the words were simple:

We are pleased to inform you...

That was it.

No fireworks.
No music.
Just a sentence.

A new life trapped in type.

She told no one.

Not yet.

She slipped the letter beneath her mattress.
Next to her notebook.

Next to her old poems.
Next to the knife.

She needed time.

Not to decide.

But to mourn.

Because every door that opens... closes something else.

That evening, Tinaye arrived.

He was humming.
Paint on his forearms.
Something in his smile still soft.

"I've painted you again," he said.

Ruramai smiled, but it didn't reach her eyes.

She handed him the letter.

Watched his face shift.

Slowly. Sharply.

"You're leaving."

She nodded.

He sat down.
Like the floor had forgotten how to carry him.

Later that night, Mama was cutting vegetables.
Precise. Silent. Ritual.

Ruramai placed the letter on the table.

Mama didn't look at it.
Didn't stop.

Then, without raising her eyes, she said:

"I knew."

"How?" Ruramai asked.

"Because I prayed for it. Before I even knew your name."

Tari was the one who asked questions.

"How high is the plane?"
"Will it rain inside it?"
"Will you write me dreams?"

"Yes."
"No."

"Always."

She gave Ruramai her stone.

"To keep the nightmares quiet."

Ruramai gave her a notebook.

"To keep your fire loud."

Fadzi came home drunk that night.

She saw the letter on the counter.
Read it.
Laughed.

Then dropped her bag with a thud.

"So they want you," she said.
"You and your fancy poems."

"You think words save lives?"

She opened a beer.
Chugged half.
Spat some.

"Let me tell you what saves lives: teeth."

Three nights later, the phone rang.

A man.
Dead.
A knife.

Fadzi.
Arrested.

No bail.

No apology.

Ruramai ran to the station.

Fadzi was in a cell with cracked walls and a smell of sweat and rot.

Her lip was split.

But she was calm.

Too calm.

"He followed me," she said.
"He touched me."
"He didn't stop."

"Then he didn't breathe."

She looked up.

"I told him no."

Ruramai didn't cry.

She felt something older than sorrow.

Recognition.

Because she knew that man.

Not his name.
But his shape.

The way he spoke to women like they owed him softness.

The way he said "Please" like a threat.

The way he looked like Gideon—

before Gideon smelled like guilt.

"I'm going to get you out," Ruramai whispered.

Fadzi leaned against the bars.

"You can't."

"Justice doesn't wear our skin."

That night, Ruramai didn't sleep.

She wrote a poem.
Then tore it.
Then wrote another.

Then a letter to the newspaper.

Then a story titled:
"What We Do With the Monsters No One Believes In."

The media found out.

Man killed in a bar toilet.
Throat slit.
Body found under a condom wrapper and crumpled beer receipt.

Woman suspect.
No signs of struggle.

"She smiled," the cop said.
"When we found her."

Ruramai visited again.

She asked: "Did you want to kill him?"

Fadzi smiled.

"No."

"Not at first."

"But he reminded me of the man who touched me when I was sixteen."

"He had the same smell."

"The same grin."

"The same belief that we're furniture."

"I snapped," she said.
"Not into madness. But into memory."

"I didn't kill him."

"I killed them—the ones that still lived inside me."

Outside, Ruramai sat on the pavement.

The street blinked.

She wrote in her notebook:

Is it murder if the world ignored the bruises?
Is it revenge if no one ever said sorry?
Is it wrong to bury what keeps rising from the grave?

She saw Tinaye that evening.

He was quiet.

Not distant.
Not cruel.

Just watching.

"Would you ever kill a man?" he asked.

"If he deserved it?" she replied.

"No. If the world told you not to."

Ruramai exhaled.

"Then yes. Especially then."

The university wrote again.

Confirming everything.

She was expected in six weeks.

Six weeks to say goodbye.

To leave behind a sister with fire in her bones.
A mother with wounds in her silence.
An aunt in a prison cell.
A man who painted her rage.
A city that chewed and spat and forgave no one.

Mama said: "Go."

Tari said: "Come back."

Tinaye said nothing.

Just kissed her wrist.

Gently.

Like a vow.

On the plane, she carried nothing sharp.

But her voice was blade enough.

She wrote one final poem on the back of her boarding pass:

I do not mourn the men who break us.
I mourn the girls we could have been.
But now—
Now I fly with teeth.

Chapter 11: We Speak in Ashes

The air in the house thickened.
Like it had secrets.
And wasn't ready to let go.

Ruramai walked from room to room.
Touching walls.
Listening to the silence.
As if the house was saying goodbye before she did.

Mama was quieter these days.
Her eyes held stories.
But her mouth held locks.

The kitchen smelled of boiled vegetables and memory.
It was always warm.
Like the only thing Mama could still offer was heat.

Fadzi's court date drew closer.

The newspapers whispered in headlines.
"Avenger or Killer?"
"Justice or Rage?"
They loved a woman in blood.
Especially when she didn't beg.

Ruramai walked through the city with her notebook pressed to her chest.
She was collecting fragments.
Faces.
Phrases.

The way pain etched itself into skin.

Tari had a fever.

"She's not sleeping," Mama said.
"She talks to walls."

Ruramai checked her forehead.
Burning.

"She needs more than I can give," Mama added.

And Ruramai knew.

She was leaving one fire for another.

Tinaye met her at the old train station.

He brought two peaches and a single sunflower.
He said nothing about the trial.
Nothing about the goodbye.

Just handed her the flower.
Bit into the fruit.
Juice on his chin.

"I'm going to miss you," he finally said.

She kissed the spot where the juice had fallen.

"I'll miss you louder."

She wrote letters she wouldn't send.

To her father: *I forgive you for making me strong through absence.*
To Gideon: *I do not forgive you. But I understand your hunger.*
To Fadzi: *I'll reside in the echoes of your pain.*
To Mama: *You were the silence that taught me how to scream.*
To herself: *You survived. Softness is a hardness that does not break.*

The court was packed.
Hot.
Hungry.

Fadzi stood straight.
No makeup.
No mercy.

The prosecutor called her a "wounded wolf."
The defense called her a "weathered flame."

Ruramai called her a woman.

On the stand, Fadzi said one thing:

"I'm tired of pretending I wasn't hurt."

Then silence.

The kind that roared.

When the verdict came, the city held its breath.

Guilty.
But not evil.

Five years. Suspended.

A miracle.

A warning.

A message:

They still fear the fire.
But they've learned to bow before it.

Later, at home, Fadzi sat in the bathtub.
Water around her like a prayer.

"I thought I'd feel free," she whispered.

Ruramai handed her soap.

"Freedom's dirty work," she replied.

The next morning, Ruramai packed.

One bag.

Two books.

Three stones.

A heart too full and too fractured.

Mama stood at the door.

"You were never mine," she said.
"Just borrowed from the fire."

They held each other.
Not tight.
But true.

At the airport, Tari cried.

"I don't want you to become a ghost," she said.

Ruramai kissed her forehead.

"Ghosts don't wear lipstick."

Then turned.
And walked.
And flew.

The sky outside the plane looked like it had been forgiven.

And maybe—
So had she.

Chapter 12: The Silence Between Lightning Strikes

The plane touched down like it didn't know it carried a storm.
Ruramai stepped onto foreign soil with borrowed courage.
Her heart, still tasting of Harare.
Her tongue, heavy with Shona prayers.

The city—new, glassy, clean—felt unreal.
Like someone had ironed out the noise.
She missed the dirt.
The smell of burning maize.
The chaos that felt like home.

The university towered like a question mark.
White walls.
Wide halls.
Names on doors she couldn't pronounce.

She was given a dorm room with a window that faced the wind.
Empty walls.
A lonely desk.
The kind of silence that dared you to fill it.

She unpacked slowly.
Book.
Stone.
Notebook.
Photograph of Tari holding a paper sun.

She placed it on the desk.
A sun in the dark.

Lectures came fast.
Thick accents.
Thin smiles.
Words like knives.

She wrote everything down.
Not to remember.
But to survive.

One girl asked where she was from.
Ruramai answered: "The inside of a scream."
The girl didn't ask again.

At night, Ruramai sat by the window.
Watched the foreign sky.
Wrote letters she wouldn't send.

To Mama: *I dreamt of you last night. You were peeling onions and smiling. Weeping.*
To Tinaye: *Do you still paint? Does your brush miss my bones?*
To Fadzi: *They don't know your name here, but I whisper it to the wind.*
To Tari: *You are my sunrise, in the night.*

She joined a poetry group.
Mostly white. Mostly loud.
They wrote about sadness as fashion.

She read one poem.
About the boy who never asked permission.
The teacher said, "Powerful metaphor."
She didn't correct him.

She left early.

There was one girl. Ana.
Curly hair. Sharp eyes. Kind voice.
She asked the right questions.
Didn't flinch when Ruramai didn't answer.

One night, over soup and silence, Ana said:
"You carry fire like it's a birthmark."

Ruramai looked at her hands.
"They burned me first," she replied.

Midterms came.
Panic. Pressure. Pages.
She passed everything. Barely.
But she was still here.
Still writing.
Still hearing Fadzi in her bones.
Still tasting Harare in her breath.

She received a parcel.
No return address.

Inside: A painting.
Of a woman standing barefoot in a storm.
Lightning in her eyes.
Sand in her mouth.

Tinaye's signature at the bottom.
She wept.

Winter came like a betrayal.
Cold crept into her joints.
Into her memories.
She missed warmth that argued back.
She missed home.
She missed the version of herself that didn't flinch at shadows.

Then came the call.
Mama's voice, trembling.

Tari. Sick. Again. Worse.
Hospital. Machines. Prayers that didn't work.
Ruramai collapsed.
In the hallway.
In her mind.

She booked a ticket.
Left everything in her drawer.
Notebook. Painting. Ana's number.
Left it all.
Except her voice.
She carried that in her spine.

The flight back was different.
Not full of hope.
Full of urgency.
Full of unfinished poems.

The hospital smelled like waiting.
Ruramai found Mama asleep in a chair.
Found Tari curled into herself.
Found God missing.

She kissed her sister's hand.
"I'm here."

Tari opened her eyes.
"Ghosts don't wear lipstick."
Then smiled.
Then slept.

That night, Ruramai walked to the rooftop.
Watched the city breathe.
Wrote in her notebook:

I left to learn.
But I return to remember.
Because what we call broken—
Was often just rearranged.

And somewhere between lightning and loss,
She finally knew:

Home isn't always soil.
Sometimes, it's the fire extinguisher we carry through the storm.

Chapter 13: Ghosts with Names

The homecoming was quiet.

No welcome songs. No ululations. Just the weight of breath and expectation.

Ruramai stepped into the house like a thief into her own life.
The couch was still by the window.
The clock still ticked off-centre.
The air was thick with a smell—disinfectant, resignation, something else.

Mama didn't rise from her chair. Just nodded, eyes swollen and dry.
Tari was asleep.
Machines beside her. Wires like new veins.
The soft beep of something trying to mimic a heartbeat.

Home had changed. Or she had.
Or both.

The neighbours stared. Not at her. Through her.
As if they saw something that frightened them.
Maybe they did.
Pain makes prophets of us all. And prophets are not always welcome.

She had left a girl.
Returned a mirror.
With cracks. With questions. With fire in her throat.

She sat with Tari. Every day.
Read her poems.

Sang old songs.
Told her stories they'd made up together.
About the moon that could cry.
About the spider whose web was mist.
About a girl who ran faster than nightmares.

Tari listened. Or seemed to.

Sometimes she opened her eyes.
Sometimes she smiled.
Other times, she looked past Ruramai and whispered, "He's here."

"Who?"

But Tari never answered.

Mama cooked less. Slept less. Prayed more.
She folded laundry like it was a prayer.
Held her rosary like it owed her answers.
Lit candles even when there was light.

"God will answer," she said.
Ruramai didn't reply.
Her silence was a type of blasphemy.
A protest in the language of the soul.

One morning, Tari said, "Do you believe in ghosts?"
Voice thin. Like faith.
Ruramai answered, "I live with them."
Tari whispered, "Me too. One sits on my chest sometimes.
He smells like old whisky and the 10 commandments."

Then she added, after a pause too heavy:
"He used to be kind."

And Ruramai did not press her.
Some truths are tombs.

She wrote.
Not in notebooks.
On walls.
Receipts.
Her own skin.

She wrote: *Some wounds don't bleed. They echo.*

She wrote: *Home is where your name is still spoken even when you are in hell.*

She wrote: *If silence had a taste, it would be the inside of our house.*

Fadzi came.

With bread. And books. And defiance in her spine.
She had cut her hair.
Wore black like it meant something.

She hugged Ruramai like a sister who had died and come back.

They sat under the jacaranda.
The purple flowers falling like apologies.

"I saw him," Fadzi said.
Her voice a dagger wrapped in wool.

"Who?"

"The one who broke her."
A pause.
"He walks freely. Laughs loudly. Eats well."

Ruramai felt bile in her mouth.
"Did you—?"

Fadzi looked away.
Ruramai finished, "—Do anything?"

Fadzi's silence was its own confession.

That night, Tari slept without moaning.
No twitches. No screams. No resistance.
Only breath.
Then not even that.

Mama collapsed to her knees.
Ruramai held her.
Not as daughter.
But as the only thing left alive.

The funeral was small.
Hushed. Tired. Grief-stripped.

No men cried.
Only Mama.
And Ruramai.
And Fadzi, her tears silent but sharp.

The priest said, "She is with the Lord."

But Ruramai thought, She is with herself. Finally.

She placed a photograph on the coffin.
Tari holding the paper sun.
The sun Ruramai had drawn with her one afternoon when laughter still
lived in them.

She whispered, "Sleep. But leave the fire with me."

Afterwards, she walked the city.
No destination. Just distance.
The wind sang hymns only she could hear.
Stray dogs followed.
And somehow, that comforted her.

That night, Ruramai climbed the roof of their house.
Held a candle.
Let the flame dance.

Then opened her notebook.

Wrote:

You burned.
I watched.
But now, I carry the fire.

And below that:

They call it survival.
But it feels like carrying a mausoleum on my back.

Chapter 14: The Things We Bury

The days after Tari's burial folded into each other like worn-out laundry.

Time no longer had edges.
Mornings bled into evenings.
Prayers grew shorter.
And the house began to forget the sound of her laughter.

Grief had its own smell—something between rust and unwashed underwear.

Ruramai stopped speaking in full sentences.
She moved like someone wading through quicksand.
Each step was effort. Each breathe a small negotiation with pain.

Mama started talking to herself again.
Sometimes in Shona. Sometimes in tongues.
She scrubbed the same floor tiles twice a day.
As if they might confess something.
As if pain could be cleaned away.

Ruramai let her be.
We all have our rituals.
Hers was silence.
Mama's was water.

Every day, Ruramai passed the mirror in the corridor.
Every day, she saw a stranger.

Not a woman.

Not a child.
Just eyes. Heavy-lidded. Haunted.
The kind of eyes that had seen too much, too soon, and too often.

She whispered to her reflection:
"Who are you when no one's watching?"

No answer.

Even her own face had become evasive.

Fadzi came back after three days.
Wore the same dress.
Carried new scars.
They didn't ask about them.

Pain didn't need backstory.
It just needed space.

They sat outside. Beneath the guava tree.
Birds above.
Ants below.

Fadzi broke the silence.

"I followed him."

Ruramai didn't flinch.
She knew who.

"He sings at weddings. Teaches at a school now. Smiles at girls."

A pause. Then:
"I wanted to stab his smile."

Ruramai finally looked up.
"And?"

"I walked away."

Ruramai's lips curled—half disgust, half relief.

"That's restraint."

Fadzi shook her head. "That's cowardice."

They both stared ahead.

At night, the dreams returned.
Not of Tari.
But of shadows.

Men without faces.
Rooms without doors.
Screams that didn't belong to her—but felt like they had been inherited.

She woke sweating.
Clutching her throat.
As if memory had fingers.

The next morning, she visited the police station.

A man in uniform asked, "What's your business?"

She said, "I want to report a man."

The pen hovered over the form.

"Name?"

She gave it.

"Crime?"

She paused.
How do you name what has no legal charge?
What do you call the theft of a soul?

"Rape," she said.

The officer's pen froze.

"And when did this happen?"

She said, "A long time ago. But it's still happening. In here."

She touched her chest.

He looked uncomfortable.

Gave her a number. Told her to wait for a call.

She never got one.

Later, Ruramai sat at Tari's grave.

There was no headstone. Just a small cross. Standing askew with arms akimbo.
Wooden. Weather-bitten. Quiet.

She read aloud from her notebook.

"You were a thunderstorm.
And they tried to put you in a jar.
But even your silence was a roar."

She left a red ribbon on the soil.
Tied it around a stone.

Fadzi had told her once:
"Every wound needs a witness."

Tari would be hers.

At home, she found Mama burning old photos.

"This one of your father," she said, holding a corner of flame.

"This one of when you were six."

Ruramai tried to snatch the last photo. Failed.
It curled into ash in midair.

"Why?" she asked.

Mama whispered, "Memories are heavy. Sometimes you have to make room for air."

That night, Ruramai wrote:

We are not only what we remember.
We are the smell in the fart.

Sunday. Church.

Ruramai wore black.

Not for mourning.
But for defiance.

The women sang. Loudly.
As if volume could resurrect the dead.

Pastor Mudyavanhu preached about Lot's wife.
About looking back.
About being turned to salt.

Ruramai thought:
I am already salt. Already burning.
What would I turn to if I turned?

When the service ended, he called her over.

"Daughter," he said, "You need deliverance."

She smiled. Not kindly.

"No. I need justice."

He didn't answer.

She wrote. On a blank page in her bible;

Men of God often struggle with truth.
When truth is man-given and not God-given.
They think that if it is not of God it must be of the Devil.
Forgetting that there is Man in between. Trapped in no man's land.

Ruramai walked home alone.
Past the cemetery.
Past the bar where boys laughed too loudly.
A bit girlish.
She thought; Alcohol brings out the feminine in men. And the masculine in women.
Better to stay sober. Even when the world was drunk. And wobbling.

She passed the schoolyard.

And there he was.

Gideon.

Smiling.
Holding a beer.
Winking at a woman who looked too young.

Ruramai stopped walking.
Time stilled.

Then she moved on.
Fast. Head high.

Because sometimes survival is not revenge.
It is the refusal to vanish.

That night, she wrote the longest poem of her life.
Pages and pages.
No structure. No rhyme.
Just breath and break and fire.

She titled it: For the Girls Who Never Came Back.

And ended it with:

If I burn, let it be bright.
If I break, let it be loud.
And if I walk away, let me be chewing embers in my mouth.
Sizzling.

Chapter 15: The Silence Between Pages

The rain came early that year.
Fat drops. Heavy clouds.
Not soft nor soothing—violent.
Like the sky had something to confess.

Ruramai sat by the window.
Notebook in hand.
Blank pages staring back.

Tari's photo lay curled at the corners.
The ink on the back had smudged.
But Ruramai remembered the words.

"Don't let them turn you into a ghost before you die."

She whispered it now. Like prayer. Like oath.

She'd gone back to the university office.
Twice.
They said her scholarship was still valid.
Her visa could be reinstated.

But she hesitated.

Not because of fear.
But because guilt is a stubborn anchor.

Mama said, "Go."

But her eyes said, "Stay."

Fadzi said, "Go find something bigger than this place."

But her voice cracked on the last word.

Zimbabwe was soil.
Blood.
Graves.
Memory.

But the world beyond—
That was a possibility.
And anonymity.

And Ruramai needed anonymity like lungs need air.

She began teaching poetry at the community center.

The girls came.
In skirts too long or too tight.
With voices soft as poisoned butter.

They didn't call it therapy.
They called it "spitting fire."

Ruramai said, "Write like you're not afraid of being understood."

One girl—Munashe—wrote about her uncle.

Another—Tatenda—wrote about a night she couldn't forget.

They cried.

They laughed.

They named their monsters.

And for the first time in weeks, Ruramai smiled without guilt.

Fadzi's visits became infrequent.
She had taken a job at a local clinic.
Cleaning, filing, and listening.

"I like the smell of antiseptic," she said.
"It makes dead things feel new."

But there was a heaviness in her limbs.
Like her body hadn't caught up with her survival.

One night, she confessed.

"I'm pregnant."

Ruramai stared at her.

"And the father?"

"Gone. Probably never real."

She touched her belly.
"I don't want to be a mother who lies."

Ruramai nodded.
That's all any of them wanted.

To not pass down silence.

Mama surprised her one evening.

"I want to see where you're going."

"Where?"

"Abroad. The university."

Ruramai blinked.

"You want to come?"

Mama laughed.

"No, child. Just show me on the map."

They unfolded the atlas.
Traced oceans. Cities. Borders.

Mama pointed.

"So this is where daughters go when their ghosts get too loud."

Ruramai didn't answer.

They both knew what she meant.

The next week, she visited Tari's grave one last time.

She brought two things: a poem and a stone.

The poem she read aloud.

"I carry your fire.
Not your ashes.
I carry your name.
Not your wound."

The stone she placed beside the ribbon.

"Stay here," she whispered.

"I have to go where you couldn't."

At the airport, she didn't cry.
Not when she hugged Mama.
Not when Fadzi gave her a notebook.
Not when the officer stamped her passport.
But on the plane—
As the wheels lifted from Harare's soil—
She pressed her forehead to the window and let the tears come.

Not grief.
Not regret.
Release.

Because sometimes the bravest thing a girl can do—
Is leave.

Chapter 16: Stillness

She stepped off the bus.
The air hit her like memory.
Dry. Warm. Familiar.
Smelling of paraffin, heat, and old regrets.
Home hadn't changed.
Not a single thing.
The pothole at the turn.
The leaning fence.
The same stray dog that might have been immortal.
She stood still.
Let the stillness swallow her.

Mama stood at the gate.
Same wraparound.
Same disapproving mouth.
But her eyes betrayed her.
They softened too fast.
"You came back," she said.
No hug.
Just a long look.
Like she was memorising something before it disappeared again.

Inside the house—everything in place.
The floral sofa.
The crooked Jesus crucifix on the wall.
The china cups behind the glass.
Even the air felt trapped in time.
Her room was untouched.
Bed made.
Curtains faded.

She touched the windowsill.
Dust curled under her fingertips.
The kind that doesn't gather in a day.

Fadzi arrived in the afternoon.
Older.
Heavier.
But still beautiful in that broken kind of way.
She brought a child.
A girl.
Small, with a stubborn mouth.
"This is Chiedza," Fadzi said.
The girl stared, then looked away.
She had her mother's quiet rage.
And something else.
Something that didn't belong to her.

They sat in the backyard.
Sun licking their feet.
"I thought you'd never come back," Fadzi said.
"I did," Ruramai answered.
"But something in me never left."
They watched ants devour a crumb between them.
Fadzi's laugh was soft.
Worn down by time.
"I told myself you'd return with riches. Papers. A man. Maybe twins."
Ruramai smiled.
"Just a degree. A voice. And I have Tinaye."
Fadzi raised an eyebrow.
"The same Tinaye?"
"Yes."
"Still boring?"

"Still kind."
They laughed.

And it felt like music from a forgotten room.

The girl played with stones.
Building circles, then destroying them.
"She doesn't talk much," Fadzi said.
"Like you," Ruramai said.
Fadzi looked away.
"She asks about her father," she whispered.
"I say he was lightning. Brief. Bright. Gone."

They visited the old tuckshop.
Nothing changed.
Same peanut butter jars.
Same sugar sold in plastic satchets.
The vendor looked up.
"Ah, the daughter of MaRuramai returns."
Word spread.
The prodigal girl.
Now a woman.
But whispers followed her like shadows.
Educated. Outspoken. Alone.

Church still stood.
So did its doctrine.
God loud.
Men louder
Women quiet.
She sat in the back row.
Let the sermon slink past her.

When the pastor spoke of submission and blind faith,
she felt her skin tighten.
Fadzi nudged her.
"Same God. Same script."
"Different Mountain," Ruramai murmured.
They left before the final Amen.

At night, she wrote.
Old words.
New truths.
Tinaye called.
"I miss you," he said.
"I'm home," she replied.
"Then I'm coming."
The thought made her chest warm.

Mama watched her sometimes.
Like one watches a candle—afraid it might go out.
"You came back with something," she said once.
"Yes. Myself."

Outside, the stars were the same.
Same constellations she'd named in childhood.
Same moon.
Everything she had left was still here.
Unmoved.
Waiting.
And maybe, just maybe,
that was the miracle.

Chapter 17: The Ashes We Keep

Ruramai stood in the library,
fingers brushing old spines.
She wasn't searching for a book.
She was hunting silence.
Thought.
Anchors.
Even now—
with her degree, her voice,
and a life unfolding—
she felt unfinished.
Like something inside her
still hadn't spoken.
She ran workshops at the college.
Women came.
Broken.
Brave.
They spoke in metaphors.
Wounds wrapped in idioms.
"My husband loves me too hard," one said.
"My brother forgets that shared orgasms do not unmake incestuous
rape." said another.
Ruramai nodded.
Took notes.
Held space.
But she never gave easy answers.
She knew the law only protected paper.
Not flesh.
Not spirit.

Tinaye visited one weekend.

He smelled of city stress.
Cologne and missed appointments.
But he held her like water—
carefully.
Like she could slip.
They sat on the veranda, knees touching.
"I think I'm ready," he said.
"For what?"
"To stop proving myself. To just be yours."
She laughed, then cried.
He held her.
Nothing was said for a long time.

Mama approved of Tinaye.
Quietly.
She watched him when he thought she wasn't looking.
Later, she pulled Ruramai aside.
"Don't run from this one."
"I'm not running," Ruramai said.
"But are you standing still?"

Fadzi baked them bread.
The child, Chiedza, played with stones.
Sometimes Ruramai looked at her
and saw Tari's eyes.
It was unbearable—
and beautiful.

She visited Tari's grave.
Took no flowers.
Just breath.
Just memory.

"I made it, sis," she whispered.
"But not whole."
Wind brushed the trees.
Somewhere a dove called.
She left nothing behind.
Only footprints.
The past no longer followed her.
It walked beside her.
Like an old friend.
Limping.
But still moving.

Chapter 18: Returning

The day she left again,
the sky was bruised with sunrise.
She wore her hair natural.
No makeup. No need to lie.
Just bare truth.
Tinaye carried her suitcase.
Mama walked her to the gate.
"Come back if you must," Mama said.
"But don't wait for us to change."
Ruramai nodded.
She didn't expect change.
She expected to change it.

The bus groaned forward.
Dust rose like smoke.
She watched the township shrink.
Roofs.
Trees.
Memory.
Her heart did not break.
It breathed.

At the university,
they welcomed her.
Lecturer.
Scholar.
Survivor.
But Ruramai knew what she really was—
a witness.

A woman who had seen the fire
and walked through.
She stood before her class.
Today's topic: *The Law and Its Silences.*
She held the chalk like a sword.
"My name is Ruramai," she said.
"I come from where justice fears to tread."
And the room listened.
The way people listen to storms.
Not with fear.
But with reverent awe.

Epilogue

That night,
in her small university flat,
she lit a candle.
The world outside pulsed with headlights and life.
Inside—
only the hush of breath
and memory.
She pulled out a notebook.
Old.
Dog-eared.
The last page was still blank.
Waiting.
She wrote.
Slowly.
Deliberately.
Each line a release.
Each word, a confession.
I loved, and I bled.
I ran, and I rose.
I spoke, and I was silenced—
Then I screamed in silence until the silence replied.
She stared at it.
Not for beauty.
But for truth.
Then—
she tore it.
Not in anger.
In peace.

She took the scraps to the sink,
lit them,
watched them curl,
darken,
become smoke.
The ashes floated.
The flame kissed her fingers.
"Go," she whispered,
"to wherever peace begins."
Smoke twisted into the night air.
Ascended like a prayer.
Or a wraith.
She didn't cry.
She exhaled.
And for the first time—
in years—
she slept without ghosts.

THE END
May 8, 2025
Domboshava
Zimbabwe

Mmap Fiction and Drama Series

If you have enjoyed *Burying Ghosts,* consider these other fine books in **Mmap Fiction and Drama Series** from *Mwanaka Media and Publishing:*

The Water Cycle by Andrew Nyongesa
A Conversation..., A Contact by Tendai Rinos Mwanaka
A Dark Energy by Tendai Rinos Mwanaka
Keys in the River: New and Collected Stories by Tendai Rinos Mwanaka
How The Twins Grew Up/Makurire Akaita Mapatya by Milutin Djurickovic and Tendai Rinos Mwanaka
White Man Walking by John Eppel
The Big Noise and Other Noises by Christopher Kudyahakudadirwe
Tiny Human Protection Agency by Megan Landman
Ashes by Ken Weene and Umar O. Abdul
Notes From A Modern Chimurenga: Collected Struggle Stories by Tendai Rinos Mwanaka
Another Chance by Chinweike Ofodile
Pano Chalo/Frawn of the Great by Stephen Mpashi, translated by Austin Kaluba
Kumafulatsi by Wonder Guchu
The Policeman Also Dies and Other Plays by Solomon A. Awuzie
Fragmented Lives by Imali J Abala
In the Beyond by Talent Madhuku
Zororo Risina Zororo by Oscar Gwiriri
Sword of Vengeance by Olatubosun David
Finding A Way Home by Tendai Mwanaka
Your Epistle by Solomon A Awuzie
The Restless Run and Ruin of the Roaches and Rats by McLayode

The Reign of Terror by Ntando Gerald
Ibala Lyabwina Nama by Austin Kaluba
Daddy, Please Don't Kill Mama by Natisha Parsons
Pilate's Angels by Goodenough Mashego
Blue threads and other stories by Matthew Kunashe Chikono
The Sylvia Plath Effect by Abigail George
The Twins by Shakemore Dirani
I, Robert's Robot and other stories by Marvel Chukwudi Pephel
Conversation With My Mother by Wonder Guchu
Stranger In Her Own Skin by William Mpina
Zimbolicious 10th Anniversary, Fictions by Tendai Rinos Mwanaka
The Kule Tokwe Diaries by Hosea Tokwe

Soon to be released

https://facebook.com/MwanakaMediaAndPublishing/